Humbug Rabbit

by Lorna Balian

ABINGDON PRESS
Nashville & New York

*Library of Congress Cataloging in
Publication Data*

BALIAN, LORNA.
    Humbug rabbit.
    SUMMARY: Father Rabbit's reply of "Hum-
bug" to the idea that he is the Easter Rabbit
doesn't spoil Easter for his children or Granny's
grandchildren. [1. Easter stories] 1. Title.
    PZ7.B1978Hq   [E]   73-9555

        ISBN 0-687-18046-5

For John, with love

This is Granny
and the house she lives in.

This is Father and Mother Rabbit
and the burrow they live in.

This is Otto, the rooster
who tells the sun and Granny
when it is time to get up in the morning.

This is Granny's chicken coop
and her hen, Gracie, who lays one egg every day.

These are the five Rabbit children.

This is Barnaby, a most devilish cat.

This is a mouse.

It is spring!
There are buds on the trees,
and tulips are peeking
out of the ground.

It will soon be Easter Sunday!

It is spring!
Mother Rabbit is doing her spring cleaning.
The floor of the burrow gets so muddy in the spring.

The Rabbit children have just heard all about Easter.
(A mouse told them.)

Granny has invited
her grandchildren to come
to her house Easter morning
for an Easter egg hunt.

HOME
SWEET
HOME

Mother Rabbit hears...

She will save all of Gracie's eggs
and color them.
They will have a grand time.

the Rabbit children ask Father Rabbit
when he is going to start laying Easter eggs.

But ALAS!

The Rabbit children believe
their father is the Easter Bunny.
(The mouse told them so.)

Gracie has stopped laying eggs!
Granny has searched the chicken coop,
and there is no egg today.

Father Rabbit tells them that that is absurd!
"There is no Easter Bunny!" he says.
"And rabbits do not lay eggs!" he says.

There have been no eggs
for days and days.

Granny is worried.

The Rabbit children are very excited!
They KNOW their father is the Easter Bunny.
(Remember what the mouse said?)

She is worried that Gracie might be ill.

She is worried that there will be no eggs for the Easter egg hunt.

Father Rabbit tells them it is all humbug.
"That mouse is a fool!" he says.
"RABBITS DO NOT LAY EGGS!" he says.

Surprise!
Granny discovers a whole nest
full of eggs.

The Rabbit children help their mother make carrot cookies.
They tell her that they will leave a plate of cookies
and a nice cup of lettuce juice on the table on Easter Eve—

(That devilish cat, Barnaby, showed her
where Gracie had been hiding them
under the chicken coop.)

She is so happy
but scolds Gracie
for worrying her like that.

for their father, who is the Easter Bunny.

Granny busily paints
and decorates eggs.

Father Rabbit tells his family that he does not
want to hear any more Easter Bunny nonsense!

"HUMBUG!" he says.
"FOOLISHNESS!" he says.

It is the night before Easter, and Granny has
hidden all the colored Easter eggs in the tall grass.
Barnaby, that devilish cat, waits until Granny
goes to bed and then pushes all the beautifully
painted eggs down the rabbit holes.

It is Easter morning,
and Granny's grandchildren arrive.
They are happy to see her
and eager to hunt
for Easter eggs.

HOME
SWEET
HOME

It is Easter morning, and there is
much excitement in the rabbit burrow.

The Rabbit children have discovered
the Easter eggs!

Granny is puzzled.
What kind of an Easter egg hunt
is this?

HOME
SWEET
HOME

Her grandchildren have looked everywhere
and have not found even one of the eggs!

Father Rabbit is puzzled.
THERE ARE EASTER EGGS HATCHING
ALL OVER HIS BURROW!

Suddenly, Granny's yard is all aflutter
with peeping chicks, hopping rabbits,
and giggling grandchildren.

Mother Rabbit shoos her children outside
to play with the new baby chicks

and tries to soothe Father Rabbit
with a quiet breakfast of carrot cookies and lettuce juice.

It is a happy Easter for Granny
and her grandchildren

and for Gracie and Otto.

The Rabbit children are so proud of their father.
They knew he was the Easter Bunny.
(The mouse told them so.)

It is the end of a lovely Easter Day.

Mother Rabbit and her children have covered their muddy floor with the colored egg shells, and it looks just lovely.

Father Rabbit is wondering if he really is
the EASTER BUNNY.

"I told you so!" says the mouse.